RESOLVING FLIGHT CHANGES

From the Debauched Squad Goals Erotica Series

M.C. Byrd

This book is dedicated to every friend that ever made it to brunch and shared salacious details over a good meal and a few drinks. The laughter and support from all those afternoons helped me to come up with this. Cheers to avocado toast and peach Bellini's.

INTRODUCTION

Grace is sitting with her friends at brunch and explaining to them her wild birthday weekend. It started with some items being left in TSA after she boarded her first flight. See how Grace handles each encounter that she has with hot men. When she finally gets to her destination she gets into some more wild fun with someone she met along her journey. Enjoy Grace on her first solo travel trip and tune in for the rest of the Debauched Squad Goals Erotica Series.

CONTENTS

SHARING AT BRUNCH

Grace was sitting with her four friends, and they had just finished listening to Malcolm's first experience sleeping with a family--his neighbors. Jacob said, "I do not think you are the king; I think your story makes you the servant. You got passed around like a hot potato."

Frank retorted, "Maybe more like a puppy. He looks happy that everyone played with him. No one wants the potato." Tracie said, "He could also just be the dirty bath water."

Grace said, "You are definitely not king. You just had a little fun." Jacob responded, "He had more than a little fun." Tracie pondered out loud, "Malcolm, do you think the three of them have done someone together before?"

Malcolm replied, "Shit. If they have, I feel cheated." The table erupted in laughter. Grace said, "Now allow me to trample all over Malcolm's *supposedly* interesting story. You will not believe what I went through to get my stuff from TSA and getting into my apartment. It was all ridiculous, but some of the dick was marvelous."

STARTING THE
SOLO TRIP

Grace was attempting to head out to the Philippines for a birthday trip; her flight was out of LAX. She lived in San Francisco and had kicked off the weekend with a CrossFit class. She was then taken out to a huge lunch with one of her friends.

Grace was going to head to LAX early to get dinner with a friend who had just purchased a gorgeous home in the marina area. She was going to spend the night with her friend, Carly, and catch up on some precious girl time.

Grace was running really late after the workout, shower, and brunch. She really wanted to nap. She figured she had enough time to still leisurely pack after her nap, but this led to Grace packing in a hurry and rushing to her job to the employee airport shuttle. She wanted to ensure that she gave herself at least an hour to get through security.

Grace also dropped by a drive-through ATM on the way to her job. She managed to drop her card while in the drive through, so she had to get out of her car and reach under her car a bit to get to the machine.

She was a flight attendant for Air California, so she could fly on her carrier for free and only paid taxes and fees to fly on other carriers. She was a bit cheap, frugal or fiscally responsible for trying to take her work shuttle instead of just calling for a ride share directly to the airport.

It was such a weird perk. She liked it because it was free, but she kind of hated it because it was not reliable. The shuttle was sometimes late or sometimes early. It really began to suck when they changed it from every fifteen minutes to every half an hour.

She was in the parking lot and parked on the front row because she managed to arrive early. She had just changed her shoes and was walking towards the pickup. The shuttle bus drove past her, and it looked like the bus sped up as she ran after it.

She decided to use a ridesharing app but she had to walk outside of her office campus because ride shares could not enter. She dragged her luggage through the exit turnstile, compared the prices in Uber and Lyft to the airport, and decided to go with Uber. The estimated wait time was seven minutes.

After five minutes, she opened the app back up to see how close the car was and to see what kind of car she should be looking for. She noticed that there was no way the car was two minutes away from its position because she could not see it.

She called the driver. "Hey, I am just trying to see how close you are. It's kind of cold out here." The driver responded, "I am just one minute away. Something is up with the app. I closed it and now it is not updating my position." Grace responded, "Okay, thank you."

Another five minutes went by. Grace is now even colder and now annoyed. She called back, but her call went unanswered. After another minute passes, and she gets an alert that the driver has canceled the ride. Grace is pissed.

She is being assigned a new driver, but they are seven minutes away. She opens the Lyft app, and they are only four minutes away, so she selects them. She looks up and sees her work shuttle pass by, and this invigorates her anger, but she does not waste energy trying to flag them down because they definitely will not stop for her outside the campus on the side of the road.

Her Lyft arrives, and she checks her bag even though her flight is within fifty minutes of taking off. It is after eight PM, and the airport security lines are fairly empty. She is not in uniform, so she does not take the known crew entrance.

She goes through general, takes out her laptop, DSLR camera and iPad. She also happened to still have her keys in her hand, so she places all of her things in a bin. Her items are rearranged a bit as she goes through security.

She gets her bag, puts her shoes back on, and heads towards her gate. She checks the monitors for her gate, and it is all the way at the end of the concourse. Grace also needs to relieve her bladder. She has to wait in line for a little bit at the counter to ask for her standby ticket.

Once it is given to her, she high tails it to the ladies room. There is a short line in the bathroom, and after she relieves herself, she sees that people are already boarding the plane. She takes her seat next to a handsome redhead guy with twinkling eyes. "I saw you were standby and noticed your crew bag. Are you traveling for work or fun?"

Grace laughed, "This will be for fun. Are you a flight attendant or pilot?" "Pilot. I was in the air force before. You?" Grace chuckled, "You aren't going to assume that I am a flight attendant?"

He broke out in a huge smile. "Assuming would make me an ass, and I try not to be a huge one." He flashed his smile again, and this time Grace could see his dimples through his sparse beard. "I am a flight attendant. Are you about to start a shift?"

"No. I am taking a few days. I feel like doing some scuba diving. I'm going to head to the Philippines or Hawaii in the morning, depending on the flights." "Cool, I am actually headed to Manilla."

"I am Jaiden, by the way." He extended his hand. Grace shook it and said, "I am Grace".

"Got any plans for Manilla?"

"No. I'm not much of a planner-- just trying to have a great time, you know. Well, I do plan to take some pictures and write a bit."

"Write about what?" he asked. Grace gave him a cheshire smile.

"I occasionally draw and write adult comics." "Perhaps, if you are into that kind of thing. Ever seen the dark side of Tumblr or Patreon?"

"Can't say that I have, is that where I can find it?" "To be honest with you-- I enjoy the anonymity of it, so I'd rather not say." "I must say, you have really stroked my interest, and I am a bit sad that you won't share, but I will respect your privacy."

It was something about the way he said stroke that made Grace want to share. She leaned into her bag to grab her iPad and show him, and then she made a loud audible gasp. "Fuck, I left my laptop and iPad at the gate!"

She popped up to talk to the other flight attendants to see if they thought security would allow the flight attendants on the next flight to pick up her items. They did not think so, especially considering all the changes to security since September 11th.

She sat back next to Jaiden, with a lot less joy than before. He gave her his card as they were landing. "Well I hope you still make it to Manilla with all your belongings."

Once they landed, she hauled ass to a quiet corner and called lost and found back in San Francisco. They told her that she had to pick up her items before ten-thirty. They would be closed afterward, and she would have to wait till the morning.

Grace said, "Please, it is my birthday. I am coming right back on the next flight tonight, but the pilots are running late from a weather delay from the east coast." She repeated, "Please, it is my birthday."

The TSA Manager said, "No. My agents have been working seventeen days into a government shutdown, and I will not have them stay a minute over."

"Please. Can I please have a friend come get it? They work for the airline too, and they will have their badge." "No, you left your security document in the bin, so it has to be you that picks it up."

Grace was *really* annoyed. She had also checked a bag, so now she needed to ask her friend to pick that up for her. She was not really sure if security would allow that.

In a few moments, Grace was on the plane returning to San Francisco from LAX, and she had spotty service. She had already missed her friend's messages asking for pictures of her ID.

Grace sent her friend the photos immediately of her ID, passport and work ID. Thankfully, her friend was able to get her bag for her. Finally, something was going her way.

Grace really could not believe her luck. The reason she needed to rush back was that she returned in the evening four days later, and she was pretty sure on that fourth or fifth day the airport mailed your stuff out to some mysterious place.

She had also committed to getting some needed writing done. Grace self-published comics as a side hustle. She also sold her photos to stock photo sites to earn additional money.

This was her first solo trip; she normally limited her travel to girls' trips if they were not for work. She usually hit it off with one other crew member and they would see sites together.

Her plane landed at ten twenty-nine. Grace ran off the plane and down to security. By the time she got there, it was ten thirty-three.

She had already been told on the phone that they would be gone at ten thirty sharp, but she asked around to see if there was any possible way to retrieve her items. The airport night manager gave her a little hope, but he came back and said that he had no access to the gate key, and Grace would need to return before 4:35 AM when lost and found picked up items.

He also warned her that lost and found did not open until 8:30 AM, and she needed to be at LAX well before her flight at 10:00 AM to the Philippines. Her first solo trip was starting to be a bust, but she did not want to give up just yet.

HEADING BACK TO HER APARTMENT

Now it was eleven o' clock. Grace did not have keys to her apartment or to her car. Her roommates were also flight attendants who were somewhere across the country for work. Grace was trying to decide if she should go home or to her friend's place that was closer to the airport.

Her friend actually did not answer after she called them twice. Grace made the decision to call her apartment complex and ask a maintenance worker to let her in. They informed her that they were not on property, and it would take thirty minutes to an hour or possibly longer.

She waited fifteen minutes before she called a Lyft home. She got into a car a few minutes later. She was surprised that it was a Lexus and said so. The handsome driver replied to her, "I normally do Lyft XL or Uber black, but it is a slow night for some reason, and I am just trying to knock some rides out."

Grace let the silence sit between them as she checked out his square jawline with an amazing full dark brown beard. He had on a ball cap but one sparkling earring in his ear. He had on very casual workout gear, including a fitted sleeveless shirt, showing off his well-defined arms.

Grace could occasionally see his beautiful eyes in the mirror, and they would occasionally flash hazel. The driver caught her staring and began to ask her questions.

"How is your evening going? This home for you?" Grace chuckled,

"My evening has been a shit show. I missed out on a great birthday dinner, and I am separated from my luggage, keys, and a few other important items."

"Sorry to hear that sweetheart, but at least you have your phone though." "I actually need to charge it. Do you mind?" He handed her the cord.

"Funny thing. If I had forgotten my phone in the bin, I likely would have gone back and got all my possessions." Grace chuckled as she thought about how true that was. Grace then thought to ask, "Do you do this full-time orrrrrrr?" She waited for a response.

He looked at her in the rearview mirror. "I just opened a jujitsu studio actually. You should come to check it out; it is only about a mile from your place-- well the address in the app. Are we headed to your boyfriend's place since you do not have your keys?"

"Well, I would hope that my boyfriend would travel with me on a fun trip or would pick me up from the airport. Turns out I do not have one, and I *would* like to check out your studio. I wouldn't mind being wrestled to the ground." She said the last part in a flirty manner, trying to give him an opening.

"What is a pretty woman like you doing without a boyfriend?" "Mostly just not willing to settle, and I am a bit busy. Mostly not looking to settle though. Unless it is one of those, *oh I need this itch scratched kind of things.*"

"Are you normally looking to have your itch scratched?" "Normally I do not have to look at all. Sometimes an interesting, handsome guy comes along and invites you to get into his car."

Grace laughs again and so did the driver; he definitely understood her innuendo. They arrive at her complex and Grace says, "I would invite you up, but I have not received a call yet from the maintenance man to say that he has arrived or that he is near."

The driver turned around and said, "What would you like to do?

Do you want me to drop you off at a bar up the street instead?" Grace thought about it for a moment. "I have another idea," as she got out of the backseat. She opened the passenger door, put her hand in his lap and gripped around his groin area.

"Well, it would help if you pulled into the spot over there that is not under a huge light, and if you could cut yours too. That would be great." He did not put up any fuss and followed her instructions rather quickly.

Grace reached over him, reclined his seat back, and moved it as far back as possible. He was almost fully erect with the anticipation of what Grace was planning to do. She pulled his dick and balls out of his basketball shorts and boxers.

She cradled and massaged his balls as she smeared his precum around the head of his penis with her other hand. Her upper body was supported by the console and her knees were in the passenger seat. She soon positioned her hand on his shaft.

She occasionally moved her hand when she deep throated him. He said, "Fuck you got skills girl!" Grace took this as a challenge. She removed his dick from her mouth, spit on it, and did an over-underhand motion on his dick and went back to sucking and tonguing the slit in his penis.

He was such a neat man. He smelled wonderful, and his pubic hairs were neatly trimmed. Grace wondered if he had a recent pussy appointment because men do not typically keep themselves so well groomed. She did not really care; she was enjoying giving him head.

He eventually worked his hand in her hair, down to her butt, and into her jeans-- under her lacy, cheeky cut underwear. He grabbed and pinched at her butt, probably leaving some bruising, and then he played with Grace's pussy. She was really into it. He played with her clit and fingered her right on her g spot.

She was totally going to cum from a finger bang in a car. They heard his phone go off with an alert for another rider; he ignored it. Her phone then went off, but she figured it was likely the maintenance guy. Grace needed to hurry up and finish this guy off.

She licked him a bit rougher, tightened her hand on his shaft, and started twisting her hand in smooth clockwise and counterclockwise motions. He didn't stand a chance with her technique and enthusiasm; he came in her mouth while she orgasmed around his fingers.

She had no interest in swallowing or making a mess in his car. When it seemed like he was mostly done, she sat up. This resulted in him pulling his hand from in her jeans. She opened the door, bent over slightly closer to the other car, and spit his cum out of her mouth.

Her phone rang again, so she opened the back door and grabbed her stuff. "Hello." "Yes-- this is maintenance. I am in the office. Are you near your apartment?"

"Yes, I am in the parking lot and will head up." "Okay" is all he said before he hung up on her. Grace thought that was kind of rude, but she was riding a bit of an endorphin high from cumming. The driver said, "Be sure to come by the studio, and we can have more than a pump and dump."

Grace chuckled, gathered her bag, and looked around the back seat for something she might be missing. "I will be sure to look you up and give you a chance to pin me."

Grace closed the door, waved goodbye, and crossed the parking lot to go up the stairs to her apartment. The maintenance man was at her door, looking pretty irritated with her.

She was kind of into his hard glare. He was over six feet tall with broad shoulders. He was not in the standard uniform, but he wore grey sweatpants, and she really liked how they fit him. He asked her for some identification, and she pulled her license out and showed him.

He looked her up and down, and she smirked. Grace was really horny after cumming from only clitoral stimulation. She really wanted some penetration, and this looked like the right guy to deliver that to her. He opened the door and said "goodnight".

She walked in, turned a light on, and dropped her purse with her foot still in the door. She pulled her shirt off revealing her breasts that were spilling out of her semi-cup bra. He looked her up and down again and walked into her apartment. She stepped back and he closed the door.

She yanked her jeans and panties off while stepping out of her shoes and other clothes. She did a little jump at him and wrapped her legs and arms around him. He dipped his head and began to nuzzle her breast.

She used one hand to lift one breast out of her bra, and he latched onto it immediately. He sucked her nipple and mouthed around her breast. She liked it so much. She pulled her tittie free of the other cup and loved the way he immediately began to lath at her other nipple.

She began to writhe against him, rubbing her clit against his groin and hip area. This made him walk towards the couch. He deposited her on the ottoman.

He pulled his wallet out of his pants and put the condom from it in his mouth. He got rid of all his clothes very quickly and dropped to his knees in front of her. He put the condom next to her then he touched her pussy lightly at first, then he stuck his finger in her pussy. "You already nice and wet for me, baby." Grace groaned.

He popped her pussy right on the clit and lips really quickly. Grace was surprised but loved it. She put her hands behind her knee caps and opened herself wider for him. She said, "yes, I am so wet for you".

Grace was actually still horny from the driver, but she loved this kind of aggression in a sexual partner. He licked her pussy, sucked on her hardened nub, then he used his fingers to spread her pussy lips open some more and speared his tongue inside.

He then licked up and down her pussy. Grace moaned, she could not believe her luck tonight. He asked her, "You ready for some dick, baby?" Grace moaned again, this time, he popped her pussy three times.

She found herself thrusting up to meet his hand for the last one. Grace said "yes, yes yes! Please put that big dick in me." He put a condom on and then proceeded to tease her. He rubbed his penis around her entrance, up and around her clit.

Grace was vibrating with excitement; she was craving his entrance. She begged some more, "Please, please let me grip your huge dick in my pussy."

He slammed into her --not waiting for her to adjust. She bucked up a little off the ottoman. He pounded into her; she could not believe how quickly his dick found her g spot.

As he thrust into her with long, fast strokes, he flicked her clit with pressure. After he felt her cum apart around his dick, he took both hands and played with her nipples. Grace loved this guy's skill; he knew exactly what to do to keep her wet, engaged and enthusiastic.

She started tightening around him with every other flick of her nipples. He pinched them all of a sudden and popped her on her clit, and she came again. He pulled out of her and sat up a little when she allowed her legs to go down.

She looked at him as he stroked the base of his penis and came into the condom. She walked limply into the bathroom, ran some warm water onto a washcloth and came back out to him. She removed the condom from him and lightly cleaned his penis. He popped her on the ass while she did this and said, "Thanks for locking yourself out".

Grace laughed really hard then. "Well hopefully I will not have to lock myself out for us to do that again." He smirked and started putting his clothes on.

"Well, you will get a survey tomorrow with my information. Be sure to give me high marks if you were satisfied with the service." He was right out of the door as soon as he was dressed again.

Grace reflected on how the last twenty hours was a bad porn plot. She traveled for a living and had never left important items in TSA --let alone an entire bin full. She managed to get to a city, realize that she left items behind, come back home, and have to be let into her apartment.

She gave her driver a blow job and had sex with the maintenance man. All this without exchanging names or having any real discussions. This may have been worse than a date from Tinder. Maybe it was better for Grace.

She could go to sleep now after she set a few alarms to ensure that she was up to get her items before Lost and Found took them. Grace woke up at 3:45 AM and took a lightning fast shower of three minutes and a few seconds. She called for another car and got dressed quickly.

BACK TO THE AIRPORT

After ensuring that she had her phone, passport, and wallet, she went down to meet her driver. No shenanigans for her this time. It was an older lady who took her to the airport. They did not talk much and enjoyed a shorter trip this early in the morning.

When she got to the airport, she printed a security document and went to stand in line at TSA. She explained what happened to an officer outside of the checkpoint and was directed where to go once she got through. She went over to this large kiosk security area and tried to tell the officer what had happened.

"Hey, I left some items here yesterday and--", she was cut off by the officer. The officer handed her a slip of paper and said, "Lost and found opens at eight thirty; you can give them a call then."

Grace took the paper. "Thank you. I have been on the phone with them but--", the officer cut her off again. "Yeah, they pick up your stuff and should be able to get you squared away."

"Thanks," said Grace "but I called yesterday and they said it should still be here from last night and will not be picked up until almost five. Did I miss them?" Grace knew she did not miss them; this guy just would not be quiet long enough to actually listen to her.

Grace wondered why she was so used to being interrupted by men. She was irked by his actions but very accustomed to it.

"What were your items again?" Grace replied, "a laptop, camera, and ipad. I think my boarding pass too." The officer chuckled, "Dang boo, you left everything didn't you."

Grace smiled and chuckled too; she did not find it funny but catching an attitude with TSA often lands a person in an unreasonable amount of conflict. As Paul Laurence Dunbar has said, "We wear the mask that grins and lies". It sometimes just makes life a bit easier to get through.

The guy made another comment and asked Grace the brand of the camera and laptop and let her sign some documents. Grace wished him a good day and hustled upstairs. She talked to the gate agent and got switched to the earlier flight time.

She texted her friend:
> Hey, I am clear for LA, pick me up, we will do breakfast and I can grab my bag from you. Thank you so much for all your help!

Grace got on her flight and was sure to check her bag again before the door closed. She reflected on the past day and wished for an amazing solo trip. Her friend was waiting for her when she got to LA. Grace was really happy to see her and cried a little in the car.

"Thank you for getting my stuff. I am really happy that I had a friend willing to do that for me and my other friends who were willing to go to the airport back home for me. It makes me wonder if I am responsible enough to travel alone considering I left some really important shit back at security before my trip even really started."

Her friend Audrey replied, "Girl you are being foolish. Of course, you're ready. This is the same as meeting up with people at a destination; you will just be meeting them for the first time while you are out. It was an accident. You do this all the time for work; you are allowed to be forgetful once."

"Eh, work is different. We basically always travel as a group. If it is a good down time then there is always at least one other crew member who will do something with me if I want."

"This will be fun, and you better stop that sniffling and get ready to enjoy your birthday weekend. But if you are worried then why not just stay and do something with friends?"

"I felt this strong urge to prove to myself that I can do whatever I want or set out to do. I felt the need to prove that my wishes were not to be tied to the whims and wants of other people." Audrey said, "This sounds like it was triggered by something a bit more. I hope you put it in your writing."

Grace did not say anything; her assumption was fairly correct. Grace was enjoying single life, but she kind of wanted to show and share her world of travel and exploration with someone special. She just hadn't found him yet, but she thought she had.

Audrey and Grace had a good breakfast somewhere close by, and she asked to be dropped off kind of early at the airport. She did not want to tempt fate and miss her flight being stuck in TSA again. She did not know how long the lines would take with the government shutdown.

BRUNCH INTERRUPTION

"Was that it? A quick free for all after a crappy night?" asked Jacob. Malcolm chimed in, "You know damn well something super slutty happened in the Philippines. She was alone several days with no one to slow her down."

Tracie added to Malcolm's sentiment, "Yeah, no one to ask her where she was going when she was getting up." Fred added, "And look at that tan; no tan lines. That means our sexy lady was out on the beach strutting her stuff."

Grace laughed, "You all know me so well. And I resent the slutty comment, Malcolm. I was just out and about, living my best life."

Malcolm said, "Bitch please. If you were busting it wide open for the uber driver and maintenance man, I know you were face down and ass up for the tanned muscled men of the islands."

CHILIN IN MANILA

Grace made it to her hotel in Manila with no issues. She checked in and went over to ask about activities with the concierge. The concierge asked her what she was looking to do.

"I want to explore a cave or two, ideally, see some whale sharks, check out one of the parks, do some zip lining, and wrap it all up with a massage." The concierge mapped out her days.

Grace had a blast doing all these activities. She met some really cool solo travelers and groups along the way. One guy was exceptionally hot. His brown beard was very scruffy and he had short brown hair with a neat cut. His curls were really loose, and his skin was sun-kissed.

She heard him speak but could not tell if he was South African or from the UK. He had heterochromia; his eyes were two different colors. One eye was a vibrant green and the other a very pale blue.

She thought he was attractive and fun but not much more than that. Then the group from the cave dive were sitting around on the beach, waiting for the boat back to Manila. It was not due for about two hours, giving the group enough time to relax as they saw fit.

They had some cups and a gallon of what can be described as hunch punch. Some people also refer to it as garbage can punch. It was basically some juices and different alcohols over fruit and ice. The group for this excursion was all roughly her age. A few of them were traveling in pairs, but most of them were all random travelers.

Everyone was pretty adventurous, sporty and very attractive. The music from the waterproof Bluetooth speaker got louder when the lively conversation began to die down. Everyone had a pretty good buzz going.

Brock, the guy with the different color eyes stood shortly after Grace. She started heading for the tree line near another cave, giving him a salacious look. Brock saw Grace checking him out earlier. If he wanted to see where this could go, it was up to him.

As Grace breached the tree line, he caught up and put his hand on her hip. "Where you headed off to, sexy lady?" Grace chuckled and thought to herself about timing and places. Only on vacation do you let such a lame line fly. It also helps that he is ridiculously hot and likes to travel.

Grace said, "Nowhere in particular. I really just wanted to see if you would follow." His face showed a little surprise in Grace's reaction, but thankfully he did not press for further conversation. He turned her into him and began to kiss her.

She opened her mouth and allowed Brock to sweep his tongue across hers. They shared a very loud kiss, and they began to run their hands up and down each other's backs. He eventually settled on her firm and round butt.

Brock decided to further their entanglement. It was really Grace who engaged; she lifted one of her legs and brought her calf up to the back of his thigh. He pulled the string loose on her royal blue bikini bottoms as she rubbed her covered clit against the hardness of his thigh.

Two people were walking towards them fairly loudly, and Brock broke their kiss to look over his shoulder at the people approaching. The guy looked very familiar; it was Jaiden from her first flight! They kept walking and could obviously see that her bikini briefs were down. They approached, the beautiful dark-haired girl with green eyes said, "It looks like your bikini is falling, need some help?"

Grace thought she was a complete idiot. The girl smirked and said, "You know, to finish taking it off". Grace smiled then, wow, someone needed to teach this girl the importance of tone and voice inflections.

The guy with chiseled abs, lightly tanned skin and blue eyes with red hair interrupted, "We would love to give you guys a hand." She loved Jaiden's timbre and his gaze on her gave Grace goosebumps. They did not wait for a vocal welcome; they continued to advance towards Grace and Brock until they had their hands on them.

Alcohol was really emboldening this situation. Grace had been kind of adventurous with sex, but this will be her first group situation. She wondered if this would count as swinging since she was not actually with Brock.

The dark haired girl pulled her top away and grasped her nipples and the undersides of her breast. She kissed Grace's neck, then her cheek. She went for Grace's mouth, but Grace turned her head. She felt like a kiss with a woman was a bit too intimate for this occasion.

Jaiden, the red-headed guy, was touching them both. He pushed his erection on the dark headed girl and had his hand down her briefs. He had a finger in her vagina while his palm was pressed against her clit in a grinding motion.

The girl began to suck the nipple of Grace and occasionally nipped her. Brock still had one hand on her waist and butt; he was also touching the dark-haired girl. Grace was temporarily lost in the sensation, but she finally began to intentionally move her hips again and rub on Brocks' chest.

She was also finally mindful that she was the only one completely naked. She removed her leg from around Brock and pulled his pants down. He helped her by closing his legs a little and stepping out of his swim trunks.

Grace and the dark-haired beauty were pleased by the length and girth of Brocks hardened penis. As Grace began to stroke his shaft, the other girls fondled his balls.

Jaiden was not to be outdone; he dropped his trunks and went to stand next to Brock. He gripped his penis with long strong strokes, and this really turned the dark-haired girl on. She dropped to her knees in the sand and immediately started licking the tip of his penis as he continued to stroke his shaft.

Jaiden got tired of her licking, so he wrapped the end of her hair around his fist and shallowly thrust into her mouth. Grace was not in the mood to give first. She leaned back on the rocks in front of the cave opening, spread her legs, and lifted one.

Grace hooked her finger in a "come over" motion towards Brock. He got closer and dipped his knees a little to suck her nipple. She pushed his head down as he got closer, so he knew to lick her pussy. Brock wasted no time; he licked at the seam of her pussy lips and then used one hand to open Grace up. He licked from above her anus to the tip of her clit.

He licked from the bottom to the top several times then settled for licking below her clit. Many women prefer a concentration on the clit, but Grace loved the kind of tongue thrusting Brock was doing to her channel.

Brock inched back up a little and lightly bit Grace's clit. She quickly came on his tongue. It normally takes a bit longer, but the moment, his enthusiasm, and the surprise of pain really took her over the edge quickly. Grace yelled out, and Brock stood and positioned his penis near her vagina. She put her hand on the tip and said, "You have a condom?"

Brock turned around and reached for his swim trunks, pulled out a pack of 3. He put one on himself and dropped the other back on top of his trunks. He fisted himself as he turned back towards

Grace.

He put his hand on her side and the other hoisted her leg up higher. He did a few shallow thrusts to ensure that she was still slick enough for him then Brock slammed into her, thrusting his body into her. His groin was constantly in contact with her clit, giving Grace amazing clitoral stimulation as well as touching her g spot while he penetrated her.

Grace could not believe her luck at finding another sexual partner she did not have to train. Grace was on the cusp of cumming again. She turned her focus from Brock at the loud noise from the dark-haired girl.

She was on her elbows and knees taking a plowing from the back. Grace had to admire the arch in her back; her breasts and shoulders were in the sand while her knees and backside were almost a perfect ninety-degree angle.

Brock regained her attention by pinching her nipple. He pulled out of her soaking wet pussy, only leaving the tip in and then slammed back into Grace. Brock dropped her leg from the crux of his arm, pulled out of her, and turned her around. Grace liked how direct he was being, but she was not super confident that she was going to like her skin rubbing against rock.

"Step back", he said into her ear, then he put one hand on her waist and pushed her shoulders forward a bit. Before she could go too far, he used one hand to wrap around her, grab a boob, and then he pressed his penis back inside her.

He only needed a few more pumps to get Grace to orgasm. As she was cumming, the dark-haired girl crawled over and said, "I want to lick her". Grace was pretty spent, and she seemed to relax a little more. Brock stepped away a bit and pulled his condom off.

He stood back about a foot with Jaiden watching the dark-haired beauty lick and kiss up Grace's thighs. She placed her hands up on Graces thighs, smearing sand on Grace. Grace thought about how this made this petite woman's hand seem kind of rough like a working man.

Grace was soon moaning fairly loudly. This woman was definitely better at this than Brock. She licked every part of her pussy with serious intent on making Grace cum. She was already kind of swollen and sensitive from the amazing sex that she just had seconds ago with Brock.

The woman licked at her labia, sucked, and lightly bit on her clit. She was even sure to lick at both sides of it. She even did this odd swirling thing with her tongue from her clit down to her anus, and she went up and down doing this a few times. Then she bit Grace's clit with a little more pressure and Grace was cumming again.

Jaiden said, "Fuck that was hot. I think you need some more dick in you now." He was already fisting his dick as he walked a couple of steps over to Grace. He picked her up and was able to slide her onto his dick while he had her legs spread with the back of her lower thighs resting on his forearms.

He was strong. Grace finally noticed how the dark-haired girl was behind him, either licking his ass or sucking on his balls from the back. Brock was behind her, and Grace stopped moaning long enough to hear how Brock's thighs were hitting that girl and also how he was slapping her on her ass.

Jaiden got her attention again. "This pussy is so fuckin tight and wet. I love your nipples." Grace liked that he said that sometimes she was a bit self-conscious about how big her nipples were.

He lifted her, pulled out of her a bit, and sucked on her nipples. His red hair was really sticking to his face now. He continued to lick her nipples. Well, the area of her areola.

Here this gorgeous strong man was, sucking on each of her nipples, worshipping them. He did the thing with his tongue where he licked one nipple really fast without putting it in his mouth then Jaiden slammed her back down on his dick and started squatting with her on it.

He was also effectively tea bagging the other girl. She had her tongue out, and he was dropping his balls in her mouth each time he squatted down. He then stood again and laid her out on the sand.

He still had her legs spread apart, so put his hands on her ankles and had her thighs brushing the sides of her stomach. He did many short thrusts quickly where his groin pressed on Grace's clit, creating the friction that led her to cumming again. He thrust deeply a few more times, and he also came.

He pulled out of her, and she sat up on her arms moments after -- just in time to see Brock pull out of the dark haired girl and cum on her butt and back.

WRAPPING UP BRUNCH

Jacob said, "Fuck. How many names of guys have you forgotten over the years?" Tracie snorted and said, "Malcolm probably only knows a fourth of the names of people that he has slept with." Frank laughed and said, "I only know because I keep a list."

Grace said to him, "Why are you keeping a list?" Frank shrugged, "Remember in sex ed when they said that if you contract something you have to tell them so they can contact all of your sexual partners," he paused for a moment.

"Well after I got chlamydia during freshman year from one of my first sexual partners, I did not want to be one of those assholes who did not tell someone they had something when they found out." Frank glanced around the table for a moment, trying to determine if he should not have shared that with his friends.

Malcolm said, "Oh, did you ever find out who gave it to you?" "No, my girlfriend and I broke up after six months, but she could have been cheating on me, and I slept with two different girls the following week."

Jacob added, "Did you tell them?" "Yeah because I did not want anyone else to run around with something and try to ignore it when it was two simple pills that would treat them."

Tracie said, "How did we go from hearing about Grace's travel debacles, to her coming upon many dicks and tongues, to talking about STD?" Malcolm replied, "I guess brunch has to get real sometime."

They chuckled then Jacob said, "It sounds like you had a good time in addition to the many dicks you hopped on. Would you solo travel again?"

"Of course" Grace said, "I had a blast! I would probably stick to cities that are pretty safe though and stay aware. I could not have done that with a friend there; they may have cockblocked."

"Or what if a friend tried to join in? That may have impacted our friendship. The point was to try it out though, so I did not feel limited to only traveling when other people were free or had the money," Grace continued.

Tracie added, "You are not going to abandon us or leave us behind on future trips are you?" Grace responded, "You know I love traveling with you all. Nothing tops memories with friends that you can reshare with."

Malcolm asked her, "Any plans to see one of these people again?" Grace blushed, "Actually yes, I really liked Jaiden. We hung out again at the bar in the hotel. Because he's a pilot with his own flight privileges, we will link up again eventually." The table erupted in laughter.

Tracie then said, "I do not think you topped Malcolm's story, but maybe you two are even." Jacob said, "Yeah, something about the twins made that a bit more debaucherous." They laughed again. Malcolm said, "I want to see you all top it."

Jacob said, "Well I am in a bit of a pickle. I have been trying something not so straight-laced." Everyone got quiet and looked at him, then Jacob added "with my admin; she is also kind of aggressive about it. A lot different from how she is at work."

ACKNOWLEDGEMENT

Thank you to Chelsea Green for sitting next to me at that reception and asking me what I have been up to. In you I found an editor and you have been a saving grace for me to finish and submit my work.

Thank you to all my friends who would ask me every month when I would release my work because they were ready to support.

Thank you very much for reading! I hope you become a subscriber at mcbyrdauthor.com

ABOUT THE AUTHOR

M.c. Byrd

M.C. has been a lover of books since she was a child and her grandmother bought her a set of 100 books that everyone should read. She mostly read her grandmas steamy novels instead.

You can find her typing away in Texas or next to you on a plane or train enjoying her next adventure.

DEBAUCHED SQUAD GOALS

Take a journey at brunch with Malcolm, Grace, Frank, Tracie and Jacob. Hear about their sexual experiences that stretch kinks and interests.

Sleeping With Neighbors

Resolving Flight Changes

My Admin Takes Control